Peter and the Waterwolf

Pippa Goodhart

illustrated by Ian Beck

With love and thanks to my teacher, Lucy Tubb — P.G.

PETER AND THE WATERWOLF
A CORGI PUPS BOOK: 0 552 54714X

First publication in Great Britain

PRINTING HISTORY
Corgi Pups edition published 2001

1 3 5 7 9 10 8 6 4 2

Set in 18/25pt Bembo MT Schoolbook

Corgi Books are published by Transworld Publishers,
61–63 Uxbridge Road, London W5 5SA,
a division of The Random House Group Ltd,
in Australia by Random House Australia (Pty) Ltd,
20 Alfred Street, Milsons Point, Sydney, NSW 2061, Australia,
in New Zealand by Random House, New Zealand Ltd,
18 Poland Road, Glenfield, Auckland 10, New Zealand
and in South Africa by Random House (Pty) Ltd,
Endulini, 5a Jubilee Road, Parktown 2193, South Africa

Made and printed in Great Britain
by Cox & Wyman Ltd, Reading, Berkshire

www.booksattransworld.co.uk/childrens

Contents

Series Reading Consultant: Prue Goodwin
Reading and Language Information Centre,
University of Reading

Chapter One

Peter lived many years ago in a
strange place where the land
was lower than the sea. It was
called the Netherlands.

"How did it get to be like
that?" Peter asked his father.

"Because people wanted more
land. For hundreds of years we
have pushed the sea off the
land. Then we've taken the land
for ourselves."

"How can you push sea?"
asked Peter. "It isn't an animal!"
His father smiled. "You're
right. The sea wasn't really
pushed. They built the huge
walls we call dykes. Then they
pumped the sea water to the
other side of the dykes."

Peter and his father were
climbing onto the top of a dyke
as they talked. At the top, they
stood and looked at the sea
moving on the other side.

"It does seem almost alive," said Peter.

"It does," agreed his father. "Some old folk even call the sea 'Waterwolf'. We have taken the Waterwolf's land. The Waterwolf wants that land back, so he wears away at the dykes with every high tide. That is why we have to keep the dykes strong.

Every stone of this dyke is helping to keep the sea off our land."

"Can we go home now, please?" asked Peter.

His father laughed. "To see the new puppy, I suppose!"

"Yes!"

Chapter Two

The puppy had arrived yesterday.
It didn't yet have a name or
know how to behave. As they
walked back home, Peter's father

told him, "You can help me to
teach the little dog. She must
learn how to herd the cows and
guard our home. But, for the
moment, she must stay shut in
the barn so that she doesn't run
away and get lost."

Peter's father went to milk
the cows. His sisters and his
mother were in the house.
There was nobody to see, so
Peter slid the bolt on the barn
door and pulled it open.

He meant only to talk to the little dog, but she ran at him.

She came bounding and yapping, and she squeezed through the gap and ran into the yard.

"Come back!" shouted Peter.
He clapped his hands and he

whistled, but the little dog was
happily chasing a flapping
flurry of chickens.

Then suddenly Peter's father
was in the yard. "Peter Dykmans!"
he roared. "Did you let that dog
out?"

Peter looked at his angry
father's face, and he turned and
ran.

"Come back here!" ordered
his father, but Peter was off and
away.

Chapter Three

Peter ran with his clogs clack-
ing over the wooden bridge. He
ran along the canal, and then
up, past a creaking windmill

that seemed to stir the wind
with its great arms. Peter ran,
panting, up to the top of the
dyke. Then he stopped and
held out his arms and let the
salty breath of the sea blow
him as if he were a ship's sail.

He looked for ships on the sea,
but there were only small fish-
ing boats. Those little boats
were hurrying for harbour as
the buffeting wind whipped the
sea to wildness. The sea is chasing the boats just as the little

dog had chased the hens,
thought Peter. He remembered
how his father had said that the
sea is like a wild dog, a
"Waterwolf". Peter looked
down at the jumping waves
lapping at the land.

"Well you won't catch me, you old Waterwolf!" Peter told it. "This dyke's too big and strong for you."

Peter picked up a stone
and threw it into the waves.

The small stone was swallowed by
the Waterwolf. Peter remembered
what his father had told him.
"Every stone of this dyke is
helping to keep the sea off our
land."

Storm clouds smudged the sky. Night was coming, and rain too. Peter looked back across the flat patchwork of fields to home.

By now his father must have caught the little dog and shut up the chickens. He would still be

angry with Peter, but the
thought of supper on the table
made Peter brave enough to set
off for home.

But, as Peter climbed
down the dyke, a
dagger of blue-
white lightning
flashed across
the darkening
sky.

It made something shine in a line down the dyke wall. Peter touched the bright line, and his finger came away wet. It wasn't raining, so where was the water from? Peter licked his finger and tasted salt. Salt!

The sea was coming through
the great thickness of the dyke!
A chill of fear ran through Peter.
The Waterwolf was coming to
get him because he'd shouted
and thrown that stone!

Peter knew that once the
Waterwolf sea had found a hole
in the dyke it would squeeze its
way through, just as the little dog
had squeezed through the barn
door. Already there was more
water pouring down the dyke.

Peter wanted to run as he had
run from his angry father, but
you can't outrun a Waterwolf
once it's loose. If Peter ran, the
Waterwolf would come splash-
ing, crashing after him,
swamping and drowning him.

Peter pushed a finger in to plug the hole in the dyke. He felt very alone and very afraid. "Help!" he called, but nobody answered.

Soon the soil around Peter's finger went soft and water seeped around it. "No!" shouted Peter.

With his free hand he grabbed
some soil from the dyke wall.
He pressed the soil into the hole.
Then he hammered it with his
fist, trying to hold back the sea
surging on the other side of the
dyke. "Help! Oh, please help!"

Already the water was washing out the mud and pouring down Peter's arms. Peter stuffed in stones and more mud.

"Help!" he shouted again. But everyone was snug in their houses with their doors shut

tight. Icy cold rain soaked Peter.
Tears burned hot down his cold
cheeks.

Chapter Four

In the darkness Peter's home
seemed to disappear. He
couldn't see it any more. Peter's
arms ached and his body shook

with cold as he pushed against
the dyke wall. He could feel
and hear the powerful, heavy
sea rising, rising with the tide
on the other side of the dyke.

Thunder roared in the sky and there was a growling too. The growling was the grinding of stones being moved by the sea, but it seemed to Peter that it was the growling of a giant

wolf. He imagined the Waterwolf, foaming and gathering, waiting to come rumbling, tumbling through the dyke to swallow him, and wallow him in waves.

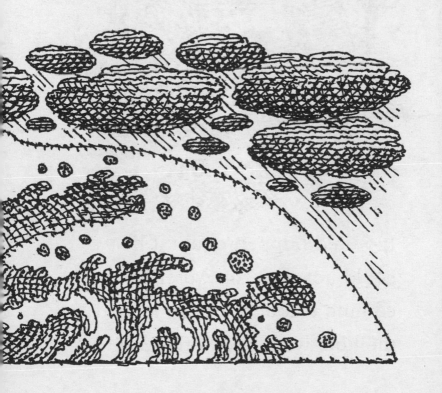

Peter had heard of floods that
had drowned whole villages.

It would happen again if he
could not stop the water from
coming through. Peter plugged
the hole with one hand, then

two, then both arms. He felt as if
his arms were in the hungry
Waterwolf's mouth. He felt as if
the sharply cold water pouring
down his arms were the
Waterwolf's slobbering teeth.

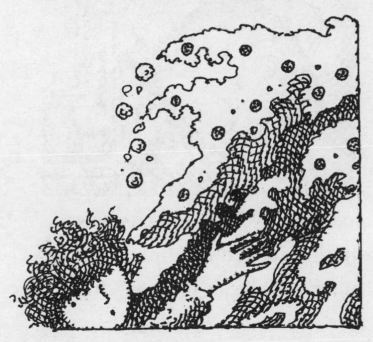

In Peter's warm home, Peter's
mother looked out into the dark
night. "Where is the boy? It's
late."

"Oh," said Peter's father. "He'll
have gone to Grandpa
Wilhelm's. I'm sure that Peter's
in no hurry to come home to a
scolding. It is his own fault if he
misses the meal."

They ate and cleared the table, all except for Peter's place. His sisters were put to bed and his mother fretted, "Where can he be?"

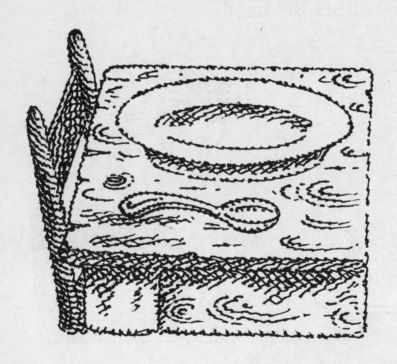

"Listen to that storm," said
Peter's father. "Grandpa will
have made Peter stay. He won't
risk the boy falling into the
canal in the dark. Peter will
come safe home in the
morning."

So Peter's mother went to bed. She shut her eyes and she prayed. Peter's father waited a while, then he silently slipped out into the stormy night.

Chapter Five

Peter's arms were in the hole
right up to his shoulders.
Freezing salty water splashed
him. He was so tired he wanted

to stop struggling and let the
Waterwolf have him. But then
Peter thought of his mother
and father and his sisters. He
thought of
the little
dog and of
Grandpa
Wilhelm.
All their lives depended on
Peter now. So Peter kept push-
ing against the weight of the

water pushing back. His clogs slipped in the mud, and he sobbed into the blustering darkness. "Please! Somebody help! I can't do it on my own!"

"Peter! Peter boy, where are you?"

"Father?" whispered Peter. A
dot of light bobbed in the darkness.
Behind the light was Peter's

father. He came running and
shouting and he caught Peter as
the Waterwolf rushed, gushing
through the hole. Then Peter's

father let go of Peter and
backed himself against the hole
in the dyke. He braced his legs
to hold back the growing force
of water.

"Run, Peter!" he shouted. "I can't hold it for long! Run and tell them to ring the bells and warn everyone!"

Stiff and numb, Peter
stumbled to his feet and ran over
the muddy fields to the nearest
house. Then he banged his fist

on the door and shouted. "Get up! It's me, Peter! The dyke is giving way and my father will be drowned!"

People grabbed for tools and ran to help while Peter ran on to wake others and to tell them to toll the bells.

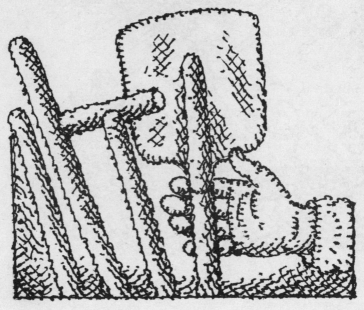

Peter ran through the village, shouting, "The dyke is giving way!

Come and help!" Then, at last,
the bells clanged loud in the
night and told Peter's message
for him.

Everyone was running through
the night to save the dyke. Peter
stumbled after them. He ran back

to where his father and the others
were fighting the Waterwolf.
They used stones and clay and
anything else they could find to
strengthen the dyke.

As they worked, the storm stilled around them. And at last the tide pulled at the Waterwolf's tail, tugging it back to sea.

 "The dyke has held!" said old Grandpa Wilhelm. "We must strengthen it some more before the next tide, but the danger is over for now."

Peter's mother wrapped a shawl around Peter's shoulders. They walked wearily home over wet fields as the sky lightened to dawn.

Chapter Six

In the house, Peter's sisters
looked at Peter with frightened
eyes as he told them the tale of
his fight through the night with
the sea.

As Peter's mother gently pulled off Peter's muddy clothes, she asked, "Do you realize what you have done, Peter?"

"I let out the dog, and Father was angry with me. So I ran away," said Peter. "You did," said his mother. "But your father forgives you. The sea never forgives. And you didn't run from the angry sea.

You saved all our lives tonight, my Peter. I'm proud of you. You were brave."

But Peter said, "There was nobody else around, so I had to stay and try and save the dyke. I had no choice."

"Maybe you had to do what you did," said his mother. "But you still did it." She smiled.

"Just think, if you had done as you were told, we might all have been drowned! If you hadn't run away, you wouldn't have found the hole in the dyke. So bad turned into good."

His mother put an arm around Peter's shoulders and hugged him.
"But that doesn't make it right

that you disobeyed your father.
There is still one chicken
missing. It will be your job to
find her and bring her home.
But sleep first, eh?"

Peter yawned. "Is the little
dog safe and well, Mother?"

Peter's father answered. "She is," he said. "But she must be trained. It won't be easy. Dogs can be as naughty as boys, you know. They don't always do as they're told! But I have an idea, Peter. You have tamed a Waterwolf, so shall we call our little dog Wolfie and hope that you can train her as well?"

"Yes, please," said Peter.

THE END